Sweetheart

Jacqueline Carmine

ISBN: 9798345528983
Imprint: Independently published

Cover design by: Jacqueline Carmine
Library of Congress Control Number: 2018675309
Printed in the United States of America

For Savana, my best friend who always makes time to read my books and provides the most valuable insight and support I could ever ask for. Thank you, Rin.

Contents

Content Warnings

Mild Obession/Manipulative Behavior
Inappropriate Workplace Behavior
Mild Harassment

Jill

"Did you forget to CC me on the monthly inventory report again, Sweetheart?" Alan asks from where he sits behind his meticulously organized desk. His amber eyes are cold and sharp as he confronts me.

The fact that my own eyes are a muddy brown in the best lighting while his are such a luminous shade only adds to my irritation.

Coming from someone else the name would be an endearment. From him it drips with condescension. Ever since he was hired, he has called me sweetheart and every effort I made to discourage it only served to encourage him. Even on memos and emails he addresses me with the nickname. The other employees think it's sweet. And our CEO, Pauline, is convinced we are dating in secret and that I need to contact HR to disclose our nonexistent relationship.

Thanks to Valentine's Day being this next Monday everything in the office is covered in pink and red decorations. And love is on everyone's mind. So naturally Pauline has sent me yet another memo to set up that meeting with HR. My grey-haired boss is a stickler for rules. She's as prim and proper as a teacher with enough smarts to take a no-name brand and build it into an empire.

It doesn't matter how many times I deny it, she's convinced we're an item. And because it clearly gets under my skin, Alan only leans into the rumor.

A pessimistic part of me believes he gets away with half of what he says and does simply because he's attractive. Tall with broad shoulders and a sharp jawline he makes every other man in the office look short and stumpy. Even O'Neill, the quality manager, who the assistants had previously dubbed McDreamy.

The fact that he's always wearing crisp custom-tailored suits with impeccably pressed dress shirts only adds to his allure and my irritation. I once wore a wrinkled blouse after a particularly rowdy girl's night and the man had the gall to offer me his portable steamer.

From anyone else it would be a friendly offer but the condescending smirk on his face taints the offer with his smug superiority.

His dark wavy hair is cut close to his ears and always meticulously styled to the point of insanity. My insanity. Everyone has bad hair days. Stroking my hand through my own brown frizz, courtesy of another humid day here in Atlanta, is yet another reminder of why I hate him. After three years I have never seen Alan Landrum less than perfectly put together. The only imperfection is a crooked smile that only adds to his attractiveness.

Just the sight of him is enough to piss me off lately.

"No Alan. It was a choice I made." I tell him with an overly saccharine smile.

"Well, I hope you don't need access to any of the Brunstein files." He replies with a pretentious smirk.

When Pauline insisted on hiring another staff member to share the workload I had handled since Everglow's creation I was hesitant to give up my responsibilities.

Pauline and I started this company from nothing. As Vice President I had a lot of responsibility and helping build a skin care company from the ground up had given me a sense of pride and if I'm honest a measure of control. I worried details would slip through the cracks and our reputation would suffer.

I was also a tiny bit bitter that he was stepping into Everglow as my equal. But in a few months that feeling faded. Alan Landrum might be a condescending jackass, but he is nothing if not thorough. I can handle petty office games and playground insults. The tradeoff is well worth it, and he has earned his place here.

I'll die before I tell him that though.

The day passes like every other before it. Alan offers me a cup of coffee when he fetches his own, the twist being that it's tepid at best. He always makes sure to do this in front of Pauline so that he appears chivalrous. It also adds fuel to the dating rumor. We attend meetings on quarterly reports and product pitches. Alan makes sure to sit closer to the presenter at each meeting and every time I shift my seat to get a better view, he is quick to mimic my movement to block my line of sight again.

This is all low-level hazing of course. Not even close to some of his more devious pranks. Like calling my mother and asking her to send me a singing telegram for my birthday because I was feeling down lately. He made sure she sent it to the office and even recommended a time when we were in a shareholder meeting. I almost killed him.

Then there was the time when he swapped my work laptop for one that was factory reset on the same day that my reports were due. I spent half the day with IT trying to figure out my passwords. All different and unique and completely unrememberable and all saved on my other computer. A computer I thought had lost all my data. Once I realized that my laptop didn't have a mangled USB port on the side, I realized Alan's duplicity. But the bastard refused to tell me where he stashed my laptop. I spent the second half of my day looking for my laptop and when I finally found it, I had to rush to get all my reports done. I didn't leave the office until 2 AM that night.

So now I consider condescension and his piss poor barista skills as normal office behavior. Hell, it's almost polite at this point.

Double checking my email, I see that Pauline does

indeed want me to work on the Brunstein files today. Smug bastard. The folder sits on his desk in open view and every so often he moves it a little to the right or to the left just to see if I'm paying attention. I do my best to ignore his little game.

Finally at noon, Pauline exits her office and I launch my plan.

"Alan?" I called a little loudly over to my coworker.

His head comes up from the paper he was reading, and I can see his eyes are narrowed. But I've gotten Pauline's attention, and he knows it.

"I just got a notification from the app that my food order is here. Could you be a lamb and go pick it up from the lobby for me?" I ask sweetly.

He glances at our boss before acquiescing and joins her as she leaves on her lunch break. I knew he couldn't refuse in front of her. Alan is all about upward mobility and rank climbing. Can't get a promotion if you are snarky and rude. At least you can't get a promotion if your boss *knows* that you're snarky and rude.

I have the file in hand a second after the elevator door closes and quickly rush to the printer to make copies. His folder is back on his desk exactly where he left it and I have my own copy before he can make his return.

When he returns empty handed as I knew he would he gives me an odd look before commenting, "Your food wasn't there."

"Oh, I forgot to order. Silly me." I say without looking up from my work.

"How did you get a notification for an order you didn't make?" He asks skeptically.

"Old notification. You know how ditzy I can be." I say flicking my hand down like I'm swatting a fly.

"Of course, Sweetheart." His deep voice rumbles and while I'm tempted to peek and see if he's smirking again, I resist.

All goes according to plan until it doesn't.

Alan

If I could have created my ideal woman, it would not be Jill Sweeny. She's gorgeous, no doubt, but I can't claim love at first sight. Lust on the other hand is another matter. Her curvy body distracted me daily, add in her mahogany brown hair that is always just a little messy and her pouty pink lips and she was the star of all my fantasies come to life.

My body desired her, but she was unrelentingly brutal, and my mind wasn't on board. Nothing like the soft and sweet woman of my dreams. My first year at Everglow was nigh on unbearable. Jill is a hard taskmaster, and her expectations are ridiculously high.

She's a perfectionist when it comes to her work, but her surroundings and personal appearance are another matter entirely. She has multiple plants at her desk and several knick-knacks adding to the cluttered space. No discernable organization system. No color coding or anything else. The disparity is enough to set me on edge.

To cope I slowly started working my way under her skin. I brewed the most bitter coffee possible and served it to her lukewarm and then I told everyone in the office that Jill preferred it that way. I switched out her laptop one day for one that was factory reset. The panic that I watched her go throughout the day as she tried to remember her passwords had me grinning from ear to ear.

I was sure my antics would get me fired. Several times I expected it. But she never reported me. Instead, she retaliated. Each action I took against her, she met with equal fervor.

That hasn't changed in the three years since my first day.

But my opinion did. Not all at once but slowly she won my respect. And then my heart. The gentle woman in my fantasies morphed from a simple sweet figure into a small woman with an aggressive attitude and a sharp tongue.

I remember the long hours she put in, staying after everyone left. The accounts she managed single-handedly, the sheer amount of paperwork that crossed her desk every day. And once I realized my position only existed to split the job she had managed to do alone for *years* she had my respect.

And that she did it without a solid support system blew my mind. I found out from Pauline that Jill's parents died when she was in her early twenties. Jill doesn't talk about it, but Pauline asked me to make sure that Jill didn't overwork herself. It became an unofficial part of my job to make sure she left the office at a reasonable hour every day. She's 100%

drive without any brakes.

Her expectations were high because she held herself to a higher standard. Everything I did she had done better. She was unrelenting because I was doing half the job she normally did, and I wasn't meeting her standards.

Never one to back down from a challenge, I rose to meet her standards and slowly I started my pursuit. The pranks lost their malicious edge, and I started thinking of her as my sweetheart. I'll never tell her but the first time I slipped up and called her Sweetheart to her face she turned the lightest shade of pink and I was fully enamored.

Now, the only person who doesn't realize I'm completely in love with her is herself. Not for lack of trying on my part.

I could tell her straight. But I don't want a flat-out rejection. Company policy says I have one chance to ask her out. Then if I ask again, it will be considered harassment, so my one shot has to count. I've watched for signs that she feels the same way I do for years.

And every Valentine's Day I do something more direct. A small signal of my affection, a feeler that I extend to see if she shares the same feeling. Like singing telegrams, or roses with poems. It's never anonymous but she treats it like a prank each time. Even the roses. The one thing I thought she would see as a sincere declaration was the worst idea of all.

She had to leave work to go to the doctor and that was how I found out she was allergic to roses.

Jill

"You know what would be super romantic?" Miranda asks from her spot perched on my desk.

I don't ask. I already have an inkling that I'm not going to like it. Every year Miranda gets lovey-dovey around two holidays. Christmas and Valentine's Day. *Every year.* Christmas is in the rear view, but the holiday of love is right around the corner. It's on a Monday, which is perfect if you want to listen to everyone cry about it not being a federal holiday.

I don't hate Valentine's Day despite what my coworkers believe. Chocolate covered strawberries are delicious and candy in all forms should be celebrated. It's the over-the-top decorations, the wistful whining of my female coworkers, and the themed pranks Alan pulls every year that I can't stand.

Last year he sent me a singing telegram. After the one he convinced my mother to send on my birthday he must have thought the prank was worth repeating. The woman who delivered it was dressed as an anatomical heart and no amount of bribery could keep her from singing *Burning Love* to me in front of the entire office. And now the video is all over the internet.

And the women at work think it was *so* romantic.

"You and Alan should fill out the relationship declaration form." Miranda says dragging my focus away from my soup and back to her.

With a round face and large glasses, she looks a little like an owl and her tendency to perch on my desk at lunch rather than pull up a chair only adds to the comparison. Her dark skin is smooth and wrinkle free despite being almost ten years my senior which never fails to make me envious. Even as a part of human resources she fights the company dress policy at every opportunity. Dresses that lean more towards casual with their colorful designs and loose fit than business appropriate.

Today she has a satin maxi dress on with large diagonal swatches of color ranging from teal and cool blue to blood red and lemon yellow. The bow at her neck has ribbons that hang down to her waist where the dress is ruched to accent her slender hips. The scarf covering her braids is made from the same pattern. Miranda's bold style never fails to make me envious but I'm not sure I could pull off the punch of color as well as she does.

"If I've told you once, I've told you a hundred times. We are not dating." I say with a frown.

Miranda and I are work friends and maybe that's why she doesn't believe me.

"Whatever you say babe." She says dismissively waving her spoon through the air like she's shooing a fly. "Have fun with your non-relationship romance but you can only dance around each other for so long before you have to admit feelings are involved."

My glower doesn't stop her rambling. If anything, it only drives her further into her delusion.

"I played the field before I met Gerald." She says twirling her spoon through the air. "I didn't think I wanted to settle down and have a family. Thought myself a free spirit and didn't want to be trapped."

She eats some of her soup and then fixes me with a stern glance, "When I met Gerald, I learned that sharing my heart with another person wasn't going to chain me down. That just because we settled down didn't mean we had to settle. And now I wouldn't change a thing."

We're almost at the end of our lunch break when she whips out her cell phone and begins showing me pictures of her son, Brayden, who is nine months old. Her husband, Gerald is a stay-at-home dad, and he sends her dozens of pictures every day.

"He knew I wanted to have a career and he volunteered to stay home." She told me. "But he also knows I have major mom guilt."

Scrolling through her phone I can admit that having a family is something I've always wanted. But dating isn't exactly my strong suit. I haven't gone on a date in well over a year. Even longer since I've had one turn into a relationship.

I know a family isn't going to fall into my lap and with my friends all settling down I'm feeling left behind. The pink and red heart streamers dangling from the ceiling mock me as I shove the longing down deep.

Alan

My lunch hour is spent with Michael and Henry from finance. They're good men and the only two people who know the truth at work. Everyone else thinks Jill and I are dating.

Because that's what I told them.

I fucking lied and I refuse to feel guilty about it. Eventually, Jill is going to come around and when she does it won't cause any waves at work. Pauline is on board, even if she's a little anxious that we haven't filled out the personal relationship declaration forms.

"You know, you could just ask her out." Michael says after finishing his salad.

He's a slim clean-shaven blonde with green eyes and a direct manner that contradicts his soft appearance.

"No, he can't" His boyfriend argues. "She'll think it's a prank and dismiss it off hand."

Henry is two inches shorter than Michael, with dark hair and a neatly trimmed beard and built like a tank. He looks like could be in the military with the muscle mass he carries but he is as gentle as Michael is harsh.

"He's getting nowhere as it is." Michael retorts. "Take your shot. If she rejects you, move on."

"You're such a romantic." I snark between bites of my sandwich. "Why do you put up with his shit?" I ask Henry.

"He's a fantastic lay." Henry quips and ducks out of reach when Michael tries to smack him.

"Look." Michael says leaning forward to stare at me. "Either date the woman or move on. These games you're playing are childish at best."

"Agree to disagree." I say before we pay the bill and head back to the office.

His heart is in the right place, and I know that. But he doesn't know Jill like I do. She's got her nose down to the grindstone and everything else is just a distraction. If I'm going to get her to see me, it's going to happen at the office.

My games keep me in her orbit and on her mind. And I will settle for that until I have her heart.

Jill

The last meeting of the day with Pauline and several managers to boot is where it all falls apart.

I start by going over the numbers of the Brunstein account and how according to my analysis we should change the serums we send to the store because sales are showing a downward trend.

Immediately Pauline interrupts me, "I'm sorry Jill but I'm not seeing what you're seeing. According to this report from Alan, our numbers on the vitality serum are climbing and so are our other formulas."

I freeze where I sit as all eyes turn on me. Even Chad, the doughy marketing manager famous for sleeping through these meetings is frowning at me. It takes me a moment to collect my thoughts before I can speak.

"My apologies. I must not have the right numbers for this quarter. Let me get back to you on this tomorrow." Each word scrapes my dry throat as I struggle not to cry in front of my boss.

Pauline nods and says to Alan, "Make sure she has the right numbers this time."

Like I need to have my work checked by a junior

employee. Her disappointed gaze pins me to my chair until another manager takes over the meeting going over a local account.

When the meeting is over, Alan and I remain seated while everyone else files out eager to head home for the day. It's not just his successful sabotage. The effort he made to alter a forty-page document. No.

It's the shit eating grin I see when I turn to face the bastard.

"Don't worry Sweetheart. I'll make sure to give you the right numbers this time. Although if you had just asked me nicely, I would have given you the original file."

It must be the blinding rage I feel building behind my sternum that causes me to bite out, "I'm done asking you for anything Alan." My tone wiping the grin from his face.

"Is that right?" He asks with raised eyebrows.

"I'm done playing your stupid little games. You were hired with one purpose and that was to make my life easier. You are a glorified assistant. An assistant that has overstepped."

"*My* games I think you mean *our-*" He begins to say but I cut him off.

"Get on your knees." The words leave my mouth and for a second, we're both frozen. His eyes are wide in shock and I'm on the verge of apologizing and running away when he pushes back his chair. His knees hit the hardwood floor of the conference room with an audible thump.

"Don't ever correct me again." I say as he looks up at me from the floor. "The games are over. Is that clear, Mr. Landrum?"

"Yes, Sweetheart." His tone isn't apologetic, but I suspect it never is. Instead, his warm baritone washes over my skin like a caress ratcheting up the tension I feel building.

I spin to face the conference table and gather my folders while Alan remains seated on his knees at my side.

"Why are you still here?" I ask without looking at him.

"You haven't dismissed me." He says in a plain tone.

"Are you incapable of the simplest things?" I ask as I spin to face him, anger curling my words into something sharp and hostile.

"You haven't released me. The only reasonable conclusion is that you still want me on my knees for you." His words carry a hint of challenge. Ire rising even further, I can't help but glare at the bane of my irritation.

"Do *not* tell me what I want." I growl between closed teeth.

"Tell me what you want." He orders, no *pleads* with a slight hitch in his breath.

There is no reasonable explanation for the next words that come out of my mouth.

"Taste me."

I wait for him to laugh. I wait for him to derisively sneer and mock me. The laughter and mockery don't come. Instead, he slides forward to pull my thighs apart. His long fingers wrap around the tops of my thighs applying the gentlest pressure to keep me open for him as he eases his shoulders between them, his hands trailing higher.

My pencil skirt bunches around my waist as his thumb rubs me through the thin fabric of my cotton panties. A second later and my panties are tugged to the side, and I could not be more grateful that I didn't wear nylons as his tongue traces the path of his thumb.

The toes of my black pumps drag on the floor as I relax back into my chair. He doesn't waste time teasing me, we both know this tension between us has been building for a long time. His mouth is warm against my pussy as his tongue alternates between slow drags and fast licks on my clit. Before I can tell him what I like he's already switching to smooth circles around my clit, and I feel my muscles tense.

His tongue slides into my pussy as I crest the edge of pleasure. Even as my muscles clench on his tongue, Alan keeps thrusting inside me and laps my dripping arousal into his mouth. The lecherous sound of him licking me with abandon causes my breath to hitch. I press my hands against his where they are still squeezing my thighs tightly.

My skin tingles as he sucks my overstimulated clit into his mouth and swirls his tongue around it. I feel my body winding tighter and tighter as he shows me no mercy. Releasing my grip on his hands I snatch a handful of his dark hair and pull him against my pussy as I grind against his face. His tongue plunges into me as he lets me guide his face, forcing the bridge of his nose against my clit. Once, twice, and on the third I tense up and come with a moan that I bite my lip to smother.

For a moment I stay seated luxuriating in the boneless feeling leftover from my orgasms. Then I make the mistake of looking at Alan. He's still kneeling between my thighs, but his trademark smirk has a shiny coating of my arousal. The chair creaks as I sit up straight and smooth my skirt down my hips. I can feel my cheeks heating up with embarrassment as I roll my chair backwards until it hits the conference table with an audible knock.

Gaze darting to where he is still kneeling, I see his smirk his gone. Perhaps the wrongness of what just happened has hit him too. He has every right to report me to HR or to Pauline. I can't believe I let myself get so carried away that I took advantage of my coworker. He was meant to help relieve my stress but not like this. We are at work. If he doesn't report me, I will have to look this man in the eye every day knowing that he gave me two of the best orgasms in my life.

My racing thoughts slam to a stop when I feel a firm grip on my knee. Looking down I see Alan looking up at me with something that could be mistaken as genuine concern.

"Time to go home." I say around the dry lump in my throat. My voice sounds dull and raspy to my own ears, but Alan doesn't comment as he regains his feet. Cleaning his mouth with the sleeve of his dress shirt as he stands, he begins gathering his belongings.

"We have a busy day tomorrow. Make sure you get some rest, Sweetheart."

He leaves the conference room without a backward glance while I try to make sense of what just happened. Alan's tongue licked and fucked my pussy like he was starving and the pleasure he wrung from my body feels better than other partnered orgasms I've had in the past. I wonder if location played a part with the thrill of getting caught ramping the tension up.

Or if it was Alan who made it more exciting. Alan, my coworker and nemesis, the bane of my existence. The man who has made every day just a little harder than necessary. Now he has all the ammunition he needs to get me out of his way.

I'm getting sacked tomorrow. No doubt about it. Glancing at my watch I grind my spiraling thoughts to a halt. It's no use worrying about the inevitable fallout.

The stress of the day melts away as I drive home. Compartmentalizing like a pro I ignore the panic that tries to crawl up my stomach to lodge in my throat. Tomorrow is for sexual harassment meetings with HR and tonight is for enjoying the blissed out feeling following in the wake of an orgasm. A hot shower and a dinner of takeout later and I sleep like a baby through the night.

Alan

Cloud fucking nine.

I was right. She wants me as much as I want her. It's been a long road, but I finally managed it. Her eyes dark with desire and her face flushed with arousal is a sight I'm never going to forget.

I wanted to take her home. To lay her down in my bed and pick up where we left off. I gave her a taste of what we can be together. I showed her how much I want to give her pleasure. When she told me to get on my knees, and I realized what she wanted, my cock got harder than granite.

It was everything I ever wanted and better than any fantasy I've had. Her taste lingers on my tongue all the way home and I savor it.

I send the files as soon as I get home. I didn't linger in the conference room or at the office because I didn't want to ruin the moment.

When I step into the shower, I think of how she looked when I left. That relaxed, sated look with her bottom lip a bright red from her biting it while I brought her to orgasm.

I replay the memory as I stroke my cock. The fury

and desire in her gaze as she ordered me to lick her pussy. The sweet taste of honey and the sound of her muffled moans.

I come with a moan of my own and I promise myself that next time we'll come together.

Jill

When I log into my work email the next morning, I'm surprised to find the Brunstein files sitting in my inbox with an actual professional memo attached.

Jill,

I have attached the updated Brunstein files for your analysis. Please let me know if you have any questions or concerns.

At your service,

Alan

Sent almost immediately after I left work yesterday, he was prompt in correcting the error of his ways. Suspiciously he addressed me by my given name. Something he never does, in person or through email. I spend a good chunk of my allotted time to get ready for work pouring over the file, checking for red flags. I learned early on while working with Alan that if something seems too good to be true, it is a setup. When I finally dash to my closet to get dressed, I forego breakfast in favor of getting to work on time, and reluctantly admit that Alan hasn't sabotaged the file.

Probably because I could forward it to Pauline as

proof that he gave me the wrong file.

One of the last to arrive at the office I'm unsurprised to find Alan, suit pressed and jaw clean shaven, sitting behind his desk tapping away at his keyboard. He was probably clocked in before the sun rose. Overachieving bastard. I am surprised to see a coffee cup emblazoned with the logo of a local coffee shop sitting on my desk next to a blueberry muffin.

"Good morning, Jill." Alan greets me with a smile, "Sleep well?"

I stare at him for a moment before taking my seat. Psychological warfare it is.

"I did. Thank you, Alan." Unable to stop at that I can't resist biting out, "Who would've thought sleep would come easier when annoying men get out of my way?"

My sarcasm seems to go right through Alan. His only reaction is that his smile stretches into a grin that highlights his dimples. Of course, the handsome bastard has dimples.

"Just let me know when I can help sleep *come* easier again." He says before turning back to his laptop.

Staring at him in silence I can't reconcile his new flirtatious manner with the sarcastic and derogatory man who has shared my office for years. My cheeks burn from his blatant double entendre.

I know it's just a new tactic to get under my skin but my knees quiver at the thought of having him lick my pussy again. I fire off an email to Pauline with my updated analysis on the Brunstein file. Glancing up at Alan I take a moment to watch him as he writes something on one of his orange sticky notes and gather my calm like an impenetrable cloak blocking out the awkwardness that is about to ensue.

"So, when are we meeting with human resources?" I ask without preamble.

"I'll message them and see when they have an opening. I'm sure they're prepped for this and will be able to see us today." He replies without looking up from his work.

"The sooner, the better." I reply, "I need to bring you up to speed on the other customer files before then."

He tilts his chin to the side before nodding in affirmation. A moment later I heard an audible ping from his computer.

"They can fit us in after lunch." He calls out and waits for my confirmation after checking our meeting calendar. He confirms the meeting via email, and I can feel the time of death for my career approaching.

I take a small sip of the coffee and I'm surprised to discover that it is a white chocolate mocha. My favorite coffee. The muffin I eat quickly because I'm hungry from having skipped breakfast. I don't care if he's celebrating his successful plan to get rid of me. It's fucking delicious.

Hours pass by quickly in the morning as I scramble to finish my reports and send them off to the appropriate departments. I have no doubt Alan can manage without me but to drop my entire workload on his shoulders while Pauline looks for my replacement would be cruel. I remember how I struggled in the years before Alan all too well.

We head to the one meeting we have scheduled before lunch, a meeting with Chad and his team to review their marketing research for the new spring product lineup.

For once Chad is alert and active in the meeting. He inserts himself into each team member's presentation to the point where every member of his staff is annoyed and aggravated.

"Thank you for your input, Chad." I say after he cuts off yet another junior member's pitch to go into a lengthy spiel about his sister's skin cancer outbreak. The pitch wasn't about sunscreen. "But I think Jamie wasn't finished pitching the rejuvenating eye cream she's been working on."

For a moment he's caught off guard. It's clear that no one on his team ever pushes back on his ego. Then a malicious smirk curves his mouth and his beady eyes lock onto me.

"You might not be aware, but I run a tight ship around here. All my reports have the right numbers at the *very* least." He chortles even as the rest of his team looks on in shame.

Fury rises from my chest but before I can find the words to dress him down and remind him that he reports to me, Alan draws his attention.

"One mistake in almost a decade." Alan begins shaking his head in disbelief, "Impressive I'll say, especially considering the mistake was due to my inability to provide the updated and corrected file. Jill has made one mistake in the lifetime of her career here at Everglow where she is a founding member of this staff. Meanwhile you're on your third strike with human resources for improper behavior and your reports are inaccurate on the off chance they are even submitted."

Chad looks shell shocked and several of his team members are hiding smiles behind their hands or looking at Alan in awe.

"I believe this is a suitable time to end this meeting. Let's reschedule this for next week on Wednesday for the same time. I look forward to everyone's uninterrupted presentations." I say holding Chad's wide eyes with my own stare. If it's the last thing I do at Everglow it will be getting him fired. "Everyone enjoy your lunch. Alan don't forget we have that meeting with HR immediately after."

"Looking forward to it, Sweetheart." Alan says as he follows me out of the meeting room.

It's only after I've shrugged on my coat and grabbed my purse that I realized Alan is waiting for me by the door.

"I was thinking about trying that new sandwich shop just down the way. Or would you prefer something heavier?" He asks.

My kneejerk reaction is to brush him off and go on my merry way to the coffee shop that makes the most delectable bear claws. But before I can summon the ire to dismiss him, I see his soft expression waiting on my opinion and I remember the way he stood up for me in the marketing meeting. Not that I needed it, but I can appreciate it.

"Sandwiches are good." I say as I wrap my scarf around my neck and lead the way out of our office and toward the elevators.

Alan

I lost my temper with Chad. I might have snapped at him even if Jill and I hadn't started officially dating. The man is on his third strike for a reason. He couldn't recognize a boundary if it slapped him in the face. And the insubordination is just a step too far.

Even when I wasn't on Team Jill, I respected her. She never asks for anything she hasn't done herself. Chad will be lucky if Jill doesn't report him to HR.

Glancing to the woman walking by my side as we make our way to my favorite lunch spot, I can't help myself.

"Are you a loan?" I watch as her eyebrows draw together at my question. "Because you have my interest.

Her mouth drops open, but no words come out. I take her silence in stride and hit her with another pickup line.

"I hope you know CPR, because you take my breath away."

She bursts into laughter, and I join her even as I rack my brain for cheesier one liners.

"Your hand looks heavy. Can I hold it for you?" I ask with a smile.

"Sure." She says before grabbing my hand and lacing our fingers together.

I didn't expect that one to land but I'm not complaining as we make our way hand in hand down the street. It's proof that yesterday wasn't a fluke. That we're on the same page and she doesn't regret giving me a chance.

We're almost to the shop when I pull her off to the side and push my luck one more time.

"Can I borrow a kiss? I promise I will give it-"

Her lips interrupt the punch line when they meet mine. Jill's fingers snake their way into my hair, destroying the hairstyle I groom to perfection every morning, but I'm not even remotely mad about it.

Our lips press and slide against each other as I wrap my arms around her waist. I have to bend down to an awkward angle but it's worth it. Her tongue slips into my mouth and the taste of the coffee I bought her this morning carries a hint of sweetness with it.

It's only when someone walking by wolf whistles that we separate.

Jill's cheeks and lips are a bright red that could be blamed on the chilly February air, but I know the truth.

We continue on our way to *O'Malley's* in silence with our hands laced tightly together and bright smiles stretching our lips.

Jill

"We are not moving in together. We haven't even had sex!" I yell in as loud a whisper as I dare from the corner booth of the sandwich shop.

With warm lighting that doesn't hurt the eyes and plenty of spacious seating, *O'Malley's* is welcoming. Clean and tastefully decorated with neutral tones, the small restaurant is better than I expected. And the tuna melt with its perfectly crisp bread on the plate in front of me is causing my mouth to water. Or it was before Alan asked me when I wanted to move into his apartment. Every other booth is filled and so are most of the tables. With so much chatter I hope our conversation won't be heard. I don't want any witnesses to this absurdity.

"Well-" He begins to argue but I shut him down quickly.

"Oral *doesn't* count!" I dismiss while smacking the table with my palm. Several people turn to look at our table, and if my cheeks weren't already on fire, I would be embarrassed enough to hide behind the table. I give them all an apologetic smile until they turn away.

"Okay. When?" He asks.

I stare at him, waiting for him to elaborate as he eats his Reuben sandwich. He finishes half before I give up waiting for an explanation he never intends to give.

"When, what?" I bite out.

"When would you like to have sex?" Alan asks earnestly.

For several seconds, my brain stalls while I try to process this auditory hallucination. Clearly this is all in my imagination. Or my dream.

"Y-You can't just ask!" I stutter out.

"Why not?" Alan asks between bites of his chips. Sea salt and vinegar potato chips, AKA the best chips in the world. His amber eyes peer into mine like he's searching for an answer and expects to find it within.

"It's not what people do." I say even as I replay our walk here. He *did* ask to hold my hand and to kiss me.

Maybe verbal consent is important to him. He's always been direct, and I don't know why I ever expected anything else when it came to sex.

"We're not people." Alan says maintaining his stare, "I have worked with you for three years and I've been in charge of your calendar for just as long. Girl's nights, trips to the nail salon, and even your doctor appointments. You schedule everything. *Everything*."

"I'm not scheduling sex!" I shout and this time when I feel people staring at me, I do my best to ignore it. They can look at me like I'm crazy. Maybe I am. But if I'm crazy then Alan is certified psychotic.

"No? Then let's set a date." Alan says before going back to his sandwich. I watch in envy as he eats. My own sandwich still sits untouched as my stomach churns with anxiety.

"A date for what?" I ask despite the feeling of certainty that Alan has circled back to his original plan.

"For you to move in with me." He says.

"I'm not moving in with you." I retort.

Glancing at my watch I see the time running out for our lunch hour. Taking a healthy bite of my tuna I watch as a wrinkle forms between his eyebrows.

"So stubborn." He mutters, "Fine. I'll compromise and settle for a dinner date this Friday. I'll add it to your calendar."

I want to protest. Tell him I have other plans. Lie about having another date even. But the heat simmering low in my belly stops me.

Reaching over I stole some of his chips. If the man wants to live with me, he can share his potato chips at the very least. The salty goodness is wasted on his crazy ass.

I have a mouth full of chips when he adds with a devilish smirk, "I won't put it on the calendar but expect to spend the night."

The bastard is scheduling sex. Damn near demanding it. The feminist in me wants to throw hands with his presumptuous ass, but the part of me that told him to kneel on the floor and eat my pussy just wants to bend over and beg for his cock.

Compromise it is then.

"Chinese." I say holding up my index finger. "My house." I say while raising another finger, "No sex." I say with three of my fingers up.

"Pizza. Your house. Sex." Alan argues mimicking my finger count.

Just as I start to argue again Alan stops me by grabbing my hand that rests on the table. His smooth palm caresses the back of my knuckles and I'm left speechless as he looks at me with a hint of vulnerability in his gaze. The moment passes and he returns to simply holding my hand. His grip is gentle but the intensity behind his stare goes hard, removing all the softness and replacing it with a wall of cold detachment.

"If you liked my tongue, and we both know you did, you'll love my cock."

Alan

I thought the war was won. Little did I know it was merely a battle. Jill hasn't realized the depth of my affection. It's enough to have me grinding my teeth. I thought we were on the same page but at least we're reading the same book.

She let me hold her hand and kiss her. She's going to file the relationship form with human resources. We're not moving in together yet but we're making progress.

Once we've been together for a few weeks, maybe a month, I'll ask again. Preferably after I've brought her to orgasm a time or two. And if she still says no, I'll just start making practical suggestions. Leave a change of clothes and a toothbrush so the nights she spends at my apartment are more comfortable. I'll stock her favorite snacks and leave clothes at her house too. Eventually her logical brain will realize that moving in together just makes sense. If she doesn't say yes but I think she will.

I might have fallen first but I know she's not far behind now. If it costs me a few chips here or there I will survive. My Sweetheart is the only person I'll let steal my food.

But I am ordering extra chips next time.

Jill

I scheduled sex with Alan.

Technically I agreed to the dinner date. I even went as far to insist there would be no sex. He agreed but the lopsided grin on his face tells me he knows I'm lying.

All the way back to the office we walk in companiable silence. Oddly enough the little voice that should be raising hell inside my head is also quiet.

It's not until we're seated in front of the human resources manager for Everglow that I realize the meeting Alan scheduled wasn't to file a sexual harassment claim. No, Miranda already had the relationship declaration forms set out.

The entire time I panicked about getting fired and Alan was planning to declare our relationship official. There is just one problem.

"We are not dating."

"Yes, we are." Alan's no-nonsense tone is back. At lunch he was relaxed but now his shoulders are stiff, and his elbows are resting on the chair arms allowing his hands to form a loose clasp in front of his blue silk tie. He's all business and I'm left bewildered.

"No, we are not."

I might have kissed him and held his hand. But I only agreed to *one* dinner date.

"What would you like to call it?"

"Perhaps a situationship?" Miranda suggests unhelpfully. Now as she peers at me through the thick lenses of her oval glasses, I can't help but squirm in my seat. The crystal chain attached to her glasses clinks against the frame as she tilts her head at me in question.

"I don't know but we're not dating." I tell her as I cross my arms in front of me. I hear a muffled huff of breath from Alan but otherwise he doesn't interrupt.

"The company does need some kind of form filled out. Just from a legal standpoint you understand." Miranda tells me with a shark toothed smile.

She's been dying to get me to fill out this form and now that I'm sitting in her office, I know she's not going to let me leave without signing it.

"Fine. We will declare our nonexistent relationship on paper." I agree just to move this meeting along. We have work to do, and if Alan isn't going to use what happened in the conference room against me, then we need to stop wasting time in the HR office.

But my mild-mannered agreement isn't enough for

him. He has to find a way to needle me, even with this.

"Legally, we are dating. Also, for future purposes we'll need a change of address form." Alan says with a wide grin stretching his lips. His perfectly white teeth on display make him look like a model for a dentistry office.

"I am not moving in with you!" I yell even as Miranda slides the form he requested across her desk. She avoids my glare and ignores my protests as Alan adds the form to his clipboard full of reports. I see her lips twitch upwards hinting at a smile, and I clutch the armrests of my chair to prevent myself from snatching the form from Alan.

"I'll need that submitted within thirty days of your move." She says even as I glower at Alan.

Miranda winking at me as we leave only adds to my irritation.

Alan

Pauline calls me into her office before I leave at the end of the day. I'm sure Miranda informed her of our visit. She's a professional no nonsense sort with her grey hair clipped into a severe bun and she wears pantsuits in every shade between grey and black with the only splash of color being her chunky necklaces. Today's selection is a canary yellow bead necklace.

"She finally agreed to go public?" She asks without preamble.

The same direct approach has steered Everglow through its first decade.

"We shouldn't see an impact on our performance. This is just a formality at this point. If anything, our interactions around the office will be less lively."

"Good." She says with a tight smile, "Because that nonsense with her laptop was a bit over the top. You both have toed the line with corporate sabotage."

"All in the name of love." I reply with a smile.

Pauline has tolerated more of our antics than I would expect from a boss. And if I didn't lie about our relationship, I'm sure she would've tolerated it less. Despite her austere appearance, she cares deeply for her employees, and much like me she is a hopeless romantic. She wouldn't be happy with my methods, particularly the lying but having Jill declare our relationship official this close to Valentine's Day makes her happy.

I'm not sure how much longer Pauling would have allowed my behavior to continue if Jill hadn't ordered me to my knees.

It's been a delicate act, flirting with Jill all these years.

She doesn't go on dates and never gossips with the other women about any of the men who work at Everglow. If she did it would have torpedoed the illusion I have steadily weaved. Her constant denial did enough damage as it was.

Jill

"Let me get this straight." Gabriella says as she sips from her glass of red wine, "He's hot as fuck, gives out orgasms like they're candy, and you want to ride his dick like it's an amusement park ride. But you don't want to date him?"

I glare at the redheaded woman lounging on my sectional. I called an emergency girl's night at my house on my way home from work and now I'm beginning to regret that decision. I've always valued her opinion but right now she's making Alan seem like a catch. Never mind all the stories I've told her through the years. She used to sympathize and help me plan my revenge schemes.

But that was before she met her husband and began trying to help my nonexistent love life. She's always been a hopeless romantic and obsessed with the holidays. Mistaking Oliver for her rideshare driver makes for the cutest story when people ask how they met. Especially when he tells his side. It was love at first sight and he claims fate and a little bit of Christmas magic brought them together just in time for the happiest day of the year. Their words, not mine.

Now my partner in crime is busy with her little family and she doesn't have time to help me plan pranks on my nemesis.

"That's an oversimplification." I say before taking a large gulp from my glass.

"No. It's really not." Gabriella argues with a pointed look over the rim of her stemless wine glass.

"Anyway." I say with a wave of my hand. I'd rather talk about anything else than my work problems.

"Just date the man." Gabriella argues immediately.

"No!"

"He wants to be exclusive and isn't shying away from commitment? In this day and age?" Emma asks with her eyebrow raised. "Marry him!"

And just like that my two best friends in the world have turned on me.

Emma and I met at a convention downtown. She was dressed head to toe in homemade chain mail made from soda can pull tabs and I was wearing a Halloween costume of my favorite videogame character Ember from *Legion X*. She was one of the few people who recognized the character by name and asked for a picture. As embarrassed as I was to have her fawn over my costume when I had bought it on clearance, I was just as enamored with her armor. The hours of dedication it took to make wowed me. We were stuck like glue for the rest of the convention and have been friends for the last five years.

"He is a condescending jackass." I say while I check on the status of our food in the delivery app. At this point I would rather watch grass grow than continue this conversation.

"Of course." Emma replies in a soothing tone, "He's a jackass who ate your pussy like a man starved."

I knew oversharing that little tidbit was going to come back to bite me in the ass. But I needed to tell someone. I just didn't think when I gushed to Emma and Gabriella that it would be used against me.

"And you already disclosed your non-relationship to human resources." Gabriella tacks on.

"Honestly it would be such a hassle to date this man." Emma replies with an eye roll.

"Such a hassle." Gabriella agrees.

Watching as they laugh and quip about my hardship brings a smile to my face. They're only pointing out the same things I've already considered.

"And really this Alan is bottom of the barrel when it comes to your potential boyfriends." Emma says as she launches into her rant about online dating. She's been trying to convince me to create a profile on the same app that she met her fiancé. "SoulConnect helped me find Andrew."

"You got lucky." I say dismissively, "You're the one percent of women who have gone out to a mountain cabin in the middle of nowhere and not become a

Law and Order episode."

Gabriella's eyes dart around the room as she tries not to get dragged into the middle of this.

"I vetted him." Emma tells me with a frown, "I told you I took precautions. And now we're getting married."

"I am so happy for you. Really, Andrew is such a nice guy. But I don't want to try online dating. I want to meet someone organically, without all the eggplant emojis and unsolicited dick pics."

Emma nods her head in a compromising manner. Before she met Andrew, our biweekly girl's nights featured a breakdown of her best and worst matches from SoulConnect. Most notably the number of couples that messaged her looking for a third to join their relationship.

We didn't find out about Andrew until she came back from a weekend away and told us that she had met her soulmate.

Precautions my ass. She didn't tell anyone that she was meeting a random stranger whose face she had never seen for sex in a remote mountain cabin. Kinky sex at that.

When she told us about the weekend, we pressed her for details. And she did not disappoint. Honestly, I still have trouble meeting Andrew's eyes to this day, two years later.

"I didn't think you would be in town this week." I say

to Emma.

She moved in with Andrew soon after that weekend and began working remotely just like he did.

"We were visiting my brother." Emma replies nonchalantly, "Andrew wants to ask him to be his best man."

"That is so sweet!" Gabriella cries from her seat on the couch.

Conversation successfully redirected to planning Emma's wedding, I breathed a sigh of relief into my glass. I love these women like sisters but I'm not ready to lie down in defeat. The pair of them are romantics at heart and they're not going to listen to my logical and sound reasoning. This is Alan we're talking about. The man who has pranked, sabotaged, and verbally sparred with me for years and would likely have continued to do so if I hadn't told him to get on his knees.

It's not my friends that Alan needs to win over. And it'll take more than fantastic sex to convince me I can trust him with my heart.

Alan

My date with Jill is an entire day away but my mind is racing. All my confidence is gone and I'm beginning to worry that I'm going to ruin what has only just begun. I let myself panic and spiral all through my dinner until I finally break and call the one person who I know will understand my predicament.

My dad answers on the second ring.

"We're dating but she's still trying to downplay our connection." I say before he can even properly greet me.

My dad is silent for a beat, no doubt collecting his thoughts before he speaks. My lack of impulse control comes from my mother. Dad is the calm in the storm that is my mother. Steady regardless of her temper. They met at work just like I met Jill. The difference being that my dad was my mom's boss at the time.

I got lucky with Jill. She isn't my supervisor despite being the person who trained me. I defer to her but there isn't any legal tape or pitfalls with our relationship. We're equals.

My parents had more obstacles to overcome than we do. But somehow, I've taken three years to get a date when it only took my mom a month.

"Give her time but also show your commitment through action. Your mother's height bothered her before we married. She was insecure that I was shorter than her and nothing I said could convince her I loved her height. Until one day I threw out every pair of shoes she owned that didn't have a heel on them."

"Mom said you tossed five hundred dollars' worth of shoes."

"I think five hundred is conservative." He said with a smile in his voice. "But it did the trick. She wore heels and towered over me for weeks. Every time she brought home a pair of tennis shoes or flats, I hid them. Until she accepted that I loved her unconditionally."

"Persistence." I say.

"Roni's my goddess but she didn't believe my words, so I showed her. Of course, now every time she misplaces a shoe, she blames me."

Jill

"A painkiller with a tall glass of water and the smell of red wine on your breath? Must have been quite the gossip sesh." Alan says as I pour myself into my chair Friday morning.

"A girl's night on a Thursday? Must have been an emergency to risk a hangover at work. Not to mention it wasn't on your calendar. I wonder what the topic up for discussion could have been?" Alan asks while looking at me with a smirk.

For the second time I notice his dimples and I hate that I notice them. Hate that he has them. As devious as he is the man shouldn't have such a cute feature.

"Shut up." I say between gulps of water.

"Did I earn their stamp of approval?" Alan asks as he brings me a second glass of water.

I want to play dumb but the earnest look on his face has me muttering the truth. As painful as it is.

"Yes."

For a blessed hour, the office is quiet. I spend most of the time catching up on emails and waiting for the aspirin to kick my headache's butt. For once in his life Alan brings me a cup of coffee that is not only hot but perfectly balanced with hazelnut creamer.

I almost checked his forehead for a fever.

By lunch I've fully recovered and I'm back to feeling like a functional human being again. Just in time for the barrage of meetings scheduled after our lunch break. Already I can feel my shoulders tensing at the mere thought of sitting in a conference room for the next four hours.

"Burgers in the park?" Alan asks when I push my chair back and stand.

I watch as he logs off his computer and straightens some papers on his desk.

"Perfect." I agree. I nearly drool as I think of a double cheeseburger with extra pickles. Greasy delicious food will even be worth Alan's dating insanity that I have no doubt he plans to subject me to.

The walk to the park is short and Alan holds my hand the entire way. Despite the lengthy line at the food truck, we get our food quickly. My double clasped greedily in my hands and Alan's bacon cheeseburger with fries in a tray he carries.

Once we spot an empty picnic table, he's quick to move the salty temptation far away from me. Perhaps I wasn't as discreet in eyeing his food as I thought.

"Don't even think about it." He says dipping a fry in a small puddle of ketchup.

I don't pretend to misunderstand.

"You want to date me?" I ask redundantly. "Share your food."

I reach for the tray, but he swiftly moves it out of my reach. I catch myself pouting and switch to a withering glare.

"If I give you some of my fries, then I'm considering this our second date." He says in his professional and clipped tone.

Despite the temptation of perfectly seasoned fries, I can't help but push back on his logic. "Tonight is going to be our first date."

"You're lucky I'm not counting that orgasm in the conference room as our first date."

I have zero doubt that my face is redder than clay and it's only the fries he finally slides my way that keep me from continuing to argue. It doesn't matter whether tonight is our first or third date. It's just semantics at this point.

We both know that unless the entire night goes off the rails then it's going to end with us naked in my bed.

Alan

It's not often that I work on personal projects during company time but it's Friday and because we're between product launches the office is quiet. All our paperwork is filed, and the marketing team is busy redesigning the spring lineup promotions. Until they have something to present our hands are idle.

So, I spend part of my day planning the perfect weekend getaway. The location is easy. It needs to be close enough to drive to but somewhere neither of us has visited. Florida overall is out. Everyone local has seen everything Florida has to offer.

I decide on Charleston, South Carolina. White, sandy beaches for me and haunted ghost tours for Jill. She's mentioned enough true crime documentaries over the years and watches too many paranormal shows not to like a ghost tour.

Not to mention the way she goes feral as Halloween approaches. Valentine's Day and Christmas she treats with apathy, perhaps even disdain. Halloween turns her into a costume critic on a sugar high from her overconsumption of candy. She goes through caramel apple suckers like each one is the last in existence.

Timing is a little tricky, but I settle for the beginning of fall. Still warm enough to swim in the ocean but beginning to hit spooky season. And far enough into the future that Jill has time to accept our relationship for what it is.

I book our bed and breakfast and add it to our calendar. A quick email to HR and our leave is approved. We'll have a long weekend together and at the end an engagement.

Jill

The night went off the rails.

It all started with our last meeting of the day. Nothing to do with the actual meeting about the Burnstein account. With the correct numbers and Alan's support it went as smoothly as possible.

No, it happened right as Pauline and the other managers were leaving. Chad came sailing through the door with a lofty smirk stretching his flabby cheeks.

"Finance cleared the expense." He says without prompting. "I've checked and the lounge is still available."

Alan and I share a confused look as we watch Pauline's shoulders sag in defeat.

"This is extremely last minute." She says in a tone that conveys her disapproval.

"Everything is approved and all we need to do is swipe the company card. My team is itching to see the Spartan's in action. Everyone will come. Even Jill and Alan will be there. Right guys?"

"Actually, we have plans-" Alan says before Chad interrupts him.

"Nonsense. This is a rare opportunity. We're talking private lounge man. And the company is covering everything."

"We won't be there." Alan says firmly. His tone goes more professional when he adds to Pauline, "It's too last minute for us."

"What a shame." Chad responds before our boss can speak, "I thought the Spartans were your team."

"They are-" Alan says before Chad cuts him off again.

"When are you going to get this chance again?" Chad asks incredulously and for once I find myself agreeing with the lout.

"We'll be there." I interject before this can drag out any longer.

The glare that Alan whips my way almost causes me to flinch.

"We can get Chinese takeout anytime. This sounds like an experience that can't be replicated. We should go." I say as the furrow between Alan's eyebrows scrunches together as he frowns at me.

"See you there." Chad throws over his shoulder as he darts out of the conference room. No doubt on his way to rope more of our coworkers into the event.

"You don't have to come." Pauline says to us but before Alan can take back my agreement, I reassure her that it's not a problem.

"We wouldn't miss it."

It's as Pauline exits the room leaving me and Alan alone that the full force of his frustration hits me with gale force.

"Our date is an experience that can't be replicated. I can watch the game from your living room if you really want to watch basketball with me."

"How expensive are lounges?"

He can't hide his wince and that settles the issue in my mind.

"We'll move our date to Saturday." I tell him and wait for his agreement.

"Fine."

"I'll meet you in the lounge."

"I can pick you up."

"If we're moving our date, I need to run a few errands. I'll meet you there."

I grip his tie and pull him forward as I raise up onto my tiptoes to press a sweet kiss to his lips.

His reluctance to reschedule our date in favor of the game only adds to his appeal. There was no doubt that he would end up in my bed tonight. But if there was, it's long gone now. And now I'm beginning to think my heart just might be ready to take a chance on him.

Alan

Fucking Chad.

Just when I think he can't be a bigger annoyance he goes above and beyond. If only he put that much effort into his actual work instead of harassing his coworkers.

A work event is *not* an ideal date by any stretch of the imagination. But the game will be over by nine and I'm sure I can take Jill out to grab a drink after. Several bars and restaurants will still be open.

Even better if her eyes are glazed over in boredom at half time, I can whisk her away sooner. Claim the experience isn't living up to my expectations. I can see a game any other Friday.

I get to the arena and the lounge early.

A few other guys are there and unfortunately one of them is Chad. I take a seat well away from him and the bastard switches seats to sit next to me. His former seatmates looked relieved at the increased distance.

The man spends a solid half hour chatting my ear off about some woman he met at the bar on Wednesday.

"Legs all the way up." He says while gesturing to his

chin. "And one hell of a rack."

He's my coworker and I don't need to stir the pot. I just keep repeating that same mantra as he continues to talk to himself. Michael and Henry join us with identical eye rolls as he starts to realize I've tuned him out.

"Miranda in human resources let it drop that you're dating Sweeny. To be honest I did not see that one coming. I thought you were a man with taste." Chad says oblivious to my glare.

"You and the scarecrow? I thought that was just a rumor! Man didn't anyone ever tell you not to dip your pen in the company ink?" Chad asks while laughing at his own joke.

I watch him for a moment, letting my fury wash through me. I take a sip of my water while I wait for him to finish laughing. Almost everyone from the office is here. I can't hit him. *I can't.*

So, I stay silent even as I want to yell and smash his beer into his face. Michael and Henry watch me with disappointment in their eyes. I get it.

But they never understood playing the long game. It won me Jill.

And now it will be Chad's undoing. I don't have to risk my position at Everglow or catch an assault charge in the process either.

Chad's been rambling for a while, and he's spilled more secrets than he is aware of. Loose lips sink ships. And his ship is taking on water fast.

I spare a glance for the room and note that Jill still hasn't arrived. I'll give it ten more minutes and then I'm stepping out to give her a call. If she doesn't plan to attend the game, then I'll just invite myself over. I don't care if she needs to run more errands.

I'd rather be grocery shopping with my sweetheart than here.

Jill

Rushing up to the private lounge Pauline rented for the game, I'm the last to arrive. Time got away from me while I was grocery shopping. I picked up way too many snack foods trying to guess what Alan might like. I also got him a toothbrush, shampoo, and conditioner. I don't know what brand of haircare he uses but he always smells minty, so I gave it my best shot.

Several of the woman, including Pauline are standing in a loose circle near a long table laden with snacks and drinks. I'm on my way to join them when I finish scanning the room and notice Alan seated next to Chad and a few of the men from finance. Lucy is there too, wearing a team jersey over her usual attire. It might be the first time I've seen her wear something so bright.

Almost all their focus is on the game playing out on the court below, but Chad is turned and talking to Alan instead of watching the basketball game.

"You and the scarecrow? I thought that was just a rumor! Man didn't anyone ever tell you not to dip your pen in the company ink?" Chad asks with a red face and a laugh that causes him to lean over gasping for air.

I wait for Alan to respond. To say anything, no matter how small. To admonish Chad. To put him down like he did in the marketing meeting.

But as I watch he just takes another sip of his drink and watches as the other man laughs.

The betrayal twists my stomach until I feel nauseous. Glancing around I see everyone is focused either on the game or the different conversations going on around the room. No one is looking at the door or at me.

Slipping back out of the door feels like I'm tucking my tail between my legs, but I can't confront him like this. I can't let anyone see me like this. Not until my shields are up and I can look them in the eye without the urge to cower.

It's only as I run into the women's bathroom that I realize tears are streaking down my face. I'm an ugly crier. I don't produce delicate tears that roll down my cheeks in poignant moments.

I blubber and have to blow my nose. It's ugly and it's messy.

But more than the swirling sadness that threatens to drag me under and consume a pint of ice cream and a bottle of red wine is the rage that simmers up. Rage that turns my cheeks red and dries my tears.

Alan Landrum wants to make a fool of me? Is ashamed of me?

I didn't help build a skin care company from the ground up just to be dismissed by a weak man with a thin ego and shitty taste in coffee. I am Jill fucking Sweeny and that man isn't worth the words needed to put him in his place.

Fuck him.

I thought he was different. That I was wrong about the last few years. I convinced myself that the vicious games and pranks were a shy man's attempts at flirting. My gut was right.

Alan is the condescending jackass I always knew he was. I should be grateful to Chad. Grateful that his poor attempts at locker room talk exposed Alan's true nature. I might not be the easiest person to love. But I know what I deserve, and he doesn't measure up.

He fooled me once and I fell for every line. Every touch and every kiss. He used me but I discovered the truth in time. I don't have the authority to fire him, but I can control how much influence he has within this company.

My revenge won't be swift. It'll be slow and steady. Let him think he's won me over. He won't be managing anything more important than the morning coffee order when I'm done with him.

He thought that little trick with the Brunstein account was clever. I'm going to have him twisted in knots with no clue where the sabotage is coming from while I play innocent.

Washing my face with cold water, I wait until my breathing evens out and then I reach into my purse and reapply my makeup. Eyeliner sharp enough to kill a man and mascara to make my lashes longer leaving me settled and calmed.

Inside my chest a storm rages with my heart beating against my ribs with a painful ache but on the outside, I am calm and professional. My brown eyes are warm even as my pink tinted lips tilt upwards in a cold smile.

Alan

She hasn't looked at me since she arrived. I was just getting ready to leave when she breezed through the door. Without a single acknowledgement my way she joined a bunch of women standing by the snack table.

Lucy from marketing joined those of us watching the game and I know from small talk around the office that she's in the minority who watch sports. But it soon becomes clear that she's the biggest fan in the room. It's thanks to her loud cheering that Chad finally shuts up. Seeing her in an oversized green jersey with the number '53' on the back over her normal black on black suit is almost comical.

I suspect she's timing her cheers to interrupt his sexist comments, especially considering she's usually timid and mild mannered, but I can't be sure. If she is, good for her. He needs to be taken down a peg or two. How the man still has a job is beyond me.

"This is going to be a tight game." Henry says trying to prompt me into commenting on the score.

I grunt in agreement but I'm far more absorbed with how Jill hasn't looked my way *once*. Maybe I should have greeted her when she came into the lounge. Just because she agreed to a date with me doesn't mean I need to stop trying to earn her love.

She's locked into conversation with Pauline and a few others. The angry pinch of skin between her eyebrows is gone for a moment while they talk. As if she senses my gaze on her she looks at me and fury is back.

All my suspicions are founded. I'll make this right, but it'll need to be after the game. She might be piping mad now, but she would be embarrassed later if we cause a scene. For the same reason I didn't confront Chad I turn my attention back to the game.

Everglow is Jill's pride and joy. I'm not going to do anything to ruin that.

Jill

All through the game I can feel Alan's eyes on me. I stand with the other women except for Lucy from marketing who is a *huge* fan. Every so often she cheers loud enough to drown out Chad's incessant comments. But the rest of the women all saw this as a social networking event rather than a sport's event and for that I am immensely grateful.

I don't know if I could sit in silence with Alan and watch a game I care nothing about. I know that without the constant chatter and shop talk that I would start drowning in my own sorrow. Pity party for one please.

The bright and cheerful smiles around me remind me of why I love Everglow. It's not just the products and the salary or the student loans that I'm slowly chipping away at. It's Miranda from human resources sharing pictures of her baby and Carol from marketing pushing back on the marketing director because the color scheme is right damn it.

And it's Pauline, who has always been a friend looking at me like she knows something is wrong despite my smile.

"This isn't mandatory you know?" She says when

she catches me alone at the snack table. A plate of chips and the tiniest number of carrots I can manage with a healthy amount of spinach dip.

"I know." I say between bites.

Is it so obvious that I would rather skin myself and crawl out of here as a slab of meat than endure another minute of Alan's betrayal? Probably for someone who has known me for so many years. But I tighten my resolve.

I'm *this* close to having Walter, the marketing director, dedicated to derailing the spring lineup, beaten into submission by his own team. Carol, his personal assistant, has my back and if I can convince Lucy, the marketing manager set to take over after Walter's retirement later this year, that pink isn't the devil then we will have enough votes in marketing to override Walter's decision. Lucy hasn't worn a shade lighter than grey since I've known her but now that I've seen her in the Spartan's jersey, I'm sure she'll come around to my freedom of expression speech.

"I could move Alan into distribution if it would help." Pauline's words catch me off guard and she quickly explains, "You haven't gone this long without speaking to each other since that time he switched your coffee for decaf."

"It was a really shitty thing to do." I murmur.

Nothing close to what he's done now of course. But that caffeine headache was something else.

I didn't return that particular prank. He got to experience working with me decaffeinated. That was punishment enough. Plus, the silent treatment once I realized why I was on a rampage. I made cookies for everyone after that. And made sure Alan got none.

"Don't move him." I tell Pauline. "I'll sort him out. Don't you worry."

I look over to where Alan is still seated and catch his gaze. We stare at each other until the rest of the room fades to a blur. I want to make him suffer but a part of me just wants to go back in time. To walk into the room five minutes later and be blissfully unaware that my boyfriend is a traitorous jerk.

Glaring at him until he turns around to watch the game should fill me with happiness, but it just leaves a hollow feeling instead.

Alan

I hop up from my seat the moment the final buzzer sounds. The guys are high fiving because our team won, and the women just look relieved the game is over.

I nod to Miranda and Pauline as I join Jill by the snack table. She fixes her gaze on the veggie tray like she can't stand to even look at me. I know she hates carrots and right now she's choosing to stare at the orange vegetable instead of me. It's the nail in the coffin. This is something more than not greeting or approaching her. But I can't ask in front of our coworkers.

I try to think of anything I did that could upset her. I didn't have any pranks planned this week aside from that last minute switch with the Brunstein file. Then it hits me.

My lies.

The blatant and direct lies I told everyone. That's the only thing that could make her this mad at me. I can only hope she'll understand my reasoning.

I couldn't sit by at work and let another man flirt with her. Couldn't bear the thought that someone would misconstrue our games for something more malicious.

Now as she finally turns to fix me with her fiercest glare, I fight the urge to melt at her feet. It's the wrong emotion. I want her passion but not like this.

"Join me for a drink?" I ask.

"It's been a long day." She replies quickly like she didn't even consider my invitation.

"I'm going to head home then." I say before tipping her chin up with my index finger.

She might hate me, but I'm going to do everything in my power to remind her why we are a good match.

A quick peck to her lips has the murderous gleam in her eye softening even if her frown still lingers.

"Goodnight, Sweetheart."

Jill

"What's wrong?" Alan asks as soon as I open my front door on Saturday night.

I thought I had played it cool yesterday but clearly not enough to throw him off my trail.

"Nothing is wrong." I reply with a sigh. "I'm just tired of marketing pushing back on the spring lineup."

Not a lie. Every spring we do the same dance at the office. Products are designed, scents are decided, promotional ads are planned, and then marketing throws a wrench into the launch at the last possible minute. Every single freaking year.

And the worst part is that it's not even Chad's fault. It's like an annual competition to see which marketing exec is going to ruin the launch.

"Walter still critiquing the color scheme?" Alan says following me into the entryway where I have him kick off his dress shoes.

Figures the man would wear a suit to a date. An at home date at that. When he drips pizza sauce on that crisp white button down, I'm not going to even offer my stain removal spray. Let the red bleed into his shirt and stain it. Nothing less than he deserves.

"I didn't know what wine would go well with the pizza." Alan says before handing me a small potted plant. "And you have several plants at your desk so I thought you might like another to add to the collection. Figured it would be better than handing you a bunch of flowers that will die in a week."

Thoughtful bastard.

"Did anyone help you pick this out?" I ask looking at the tear-drop shaped leaves in a gorgeous blue-green shade.

"Yeah, the guy at the store said it was low maintenance." Alan says before stuffing his hands into the pockets of his slacks and rocking back onto his heels for a moment. "Do you not like it?"

"I love it." I admit before I ask my next question. "Did the man seem irritated with you?"

I watch as Alan stares at a spot on my living room floor for several moments. His eyebrows furrowed and I know the answer before he looks up to tell me that the man was indeed irritated.

"He seemed to be having a bad day." Alan said with a frown. "I was asking about buying my girlfriend a plant and he told me his wife had just left him."

"This plant." I say holding it up for his inspection. "It's called Donkey's Tail."

We stare at each other for a moment and then bit by bit we both start to crack. I dissolve into laughter first. Alan not far behind.

"He was calling you a jackass!" I shout.

"Man didn't even know me! All I wanted was a recommendation." Alan replies with a bright smile stretching his face.

"Well, you're in luck, because I don't have one of these yet." I say once I catch my breath.

Leading him through the house I show him the kitchen and then stepping out my back door I let him take in my mini greenhouse. It's not much. Just some polycarbonate sheets attached to the siding my house so that every time I step into my backyard I walk through rows of my healthy plants. The rest of the yard visible from inside the clear walls isn't very impressive. Boring grass that I have to cut every other week in the summer.

If Mr. Porter next door is to be believed I should be cutting it weekly. But that is not going to happen.

"You have more plants than the store did!" Alan's voice rings through the space and I have to muffle my laugh. "Do you swear you don't have that one? You have literally all the others I considered."

"I swear." I say with a hand to my heart. "You found the perfect plant for me."

He watches me with suspicion as I find a spot for my new plant. I'll need to repot it tomorrow but for now it can be shelved without worry. The blue pot it came in is only a little too small for its size and I have plenty of bigger planters to use. I get so swept up trying to decide which hanging pot I will use that I don't notice when Alan moves behind me.

"The one plant you didn't have?" He asks before sweeping my hair to the side. "Fate seems to be on my side."

I try to ignore the burning heat that his kisses ignite. Every lick and nibble from my throat to my shoulder where he has swept my sweater out of his way makes me want to forget his deception. At least for a night.

"You got lucky." I moan as he pulls back, his warmth leaving me abruptly.

"No, Sweetheart. I've got more than luck on my side." He takes my hand and leads me back into my house like he's the host and not the other way around. "Especially once I consider how prickly you've been this weekend."

"I have not been prickly." I protest.

"Yes, you have." He replies immediately, "There was no reason to postpone our date. The game didn't matter and there was still plenty of time after to have dinner or even catch a movie. I kept checking my phone all day just to make sure you didn't get cold feet and cancel this date too."

"Luxury lounge seemed like a once in a lifetime thing." I muttered looking away from his accusatory glare.

"If *Chad* can get Pauline and finances on board, I think I can do the same."

"I was tired." I argue and without waiting for a response because I can tell by the clenching of his jaw that he has one locked and loaded I grab my phone off the kitchen table and call in our order to the local pizza place. Three years of working together and the quarterly pizza parties ensures I know what toppings he likes.

"As I was saying." Alan says as soon as I hang up, "Prickly little cactus."

His finger playfully poking me in my collarbone is enough for me to snap.

"You!" I shout at him while jabbing my own finger into his chest. "You let that stupid man talk about me like I was a conquest!"

The anger in Alan's eyes disappears and I watch him try to piece the puzzle together of why I am mad at him. It only makes me more furious.

"A scarecrow?" I yell poking him in the chest to punctuate every word. "Is that what the men who work at Everglow call me?"

I watch as his lips move but no sound comes out.

"Get out of my home." I say with a raspy voice. "Get the fuck out right now."

For a moment he doesn't move but then when I go to start yelling again, he holds up his hands like he's surrendering, and he leaves. Just like that and he's gone.

No words to defend himself. Because everything I thought was true. He is ashamed of me. Using me to get further in the company.

My throat feels sore and raw, and my vision is blurry from the tears. I'm almost in my bedroom when the doorbell rings.

The pizza. I know it's the delivery driver but that doesn't stop me from hoping that it's Alan. That he has an excuse or an explanation. Anything to ease this hurt in my heart.

But when I open the door, the lanky kid holding the stack of pizza boxes is the only person to greet me.

"Dude already paid." The teen says when I go to hand him the cash. "Tip too. Hope your day gets better."

The pity of a teenager is what truly sends me under. To be so pathetic that I fell for Alan and his lies is bad enough. To let him break my heart and leave it open for everyone to see is worse. Monday I will be back to myself. But it's Saturday night, I don't have to see another soul this weekend and I have three pizzas to myself. Even if one has a disgusting amount of pineapple on it.

Alan

It's so much worse than my lies to our coworkers. The ruse I orchestrated at work pales in comparison to the true betrayal.

I should've fucking hit him.

She's lost all faith in me. My sweetheart has turned bitter, and I don't know how to fix it. I never should have let him talk about her. Pauline was right there. I could've reported him on the spot, damn the scene it would cause.

If Jill heard his commentary, then I'm sure most of the others did too. I let my woman down.

Just when everything I ever dreamed to crave was within my reach, I fucked it all up. The entire drive to my apartment my mind is a tangled mess. I had so many chances to right this wrong.

At the very least I could've confronted him. Told him not to talk about my girlfriend. Insulted him. Told him Jill is a goddess he could never dream of dating. That no one of sound mind would ever choose a pathetic toad like him.

The dagger that drives it deep. If I let him feel comfortable to say these things in my company, then I'm no better than him. If he's a sexist chauvinistic pig, then so am I.

Does it even end with Jill? Lucy was there too. The only woman who felt comfortable enough to join us. Because of Chad she had to shout over him to avoid listening to his rhetoric. Just to enjoy a single basketball game. And she works in his department. How many meetings has she had to attend and listen to his comments?

When I get home, I send an email to HR. An official complaint detailing Chad's comments Friday night and his insubordinate behavior at the Thursday meeting.

It's too little too late. I know it is.

But it's a start.

Tomorrow I'll go back to Jill's house first thing. I'll get down on my knees if I have to beg her to take me back. She's the sun to my earth and I can't give up until she knows that I'll do *anything* to fix this.

The temptation to drink my blues away arises but I don't give in to it. It'll only be a bandage, it can't heal the hurt.

Sitting on my couch I replay the fight. I didn't say anything. Nothing in my defense, nothing to reassure her. I've left her crying and that is what keeps me up all night.

I have no defense and I let her down. But I shouldn't have walked away. She ordered me out of her house, but I could have stood on her porch and apologized. Begged her forgiveness.

The only thought bringing me comfort is the soft easiness we had before the fight. Jill letting me into her house and accepting my gift. Those mind melting kisses that had me forgetting the prickly behavior from the night before.

As the hours tick by my vision blurs and I'm not shocked to find myself crying. When the sky turns pink with the first hint of a sunrise, I grab my keys. It's too damn early for a Sunday but I can't wait another minute.

I gave her space. Now I need her to give me a chance.

Jill

My mope lasts until I fall asleep on my couch early Sunday morning. Everything I try to do only makes me think of Alan. In the most bizarre ways. Working together for as long as we have meant a lot of small talk. Insignificant details that I can't forget. Like how much he hated reality TV shows. I can't watch someone else's life fall apart without thinking of him. Even if the drama is one hundred percent staged.

I can't even think about touching the Hawaiian pizza still sitting on my kitchen counter. I play videogames until I fall asleep.

A loud banging sound wakes me up. Hair in disarray with several pieces sticking to my face where I've no doubt drooled in my sleep I stumble to my feet. The blanket I wrapped myself into a human burrito with tangles with my feet and nearly sends me to the ground. My knee bangs into the coffee table in front of my sofa in my hurry.

The banging resumes and I realize someone is at my front door. A quick glance at my phone shows it is only six in the morning. I consider the texts I sent Gabriella and Emma last night, pouring out my misery and realize it's one or both coming to share in my woes.

It's only after I open the door to see Alan standing on my porch that I realize I should have looked through the peep hole first. My hand goes to my messy hair automatically before I take in his rumpled appearance.

He's still in the same clothes as last night. The same suit and tie although his hair is a mess sticking up in odd directions and his tie is hanging loosely from his shirt collar which is unbuttoned. Even in a wrinkled suit he still looks better than I do. Even with red rimmed eyes he still looks like sex in a suit, and it should be enough to piss me off but all it does is send a pang of longing into my chest.

I wanted him to hurt as much as I do. And now that the damage is done, I just want to take it all back. I want to march up to him in that game and confront him on the spot. And hope that he says something that doesn't break me into pieces.

We take each other in and without a word I let him into the house. I don't need to wake any of my neighbors up at this ungodly hour on a Sunday morning by yelling at a man in my front yard.

He goes straight through my living room and back to the kitchen. I see him glance out my back door and knowing exactly what he's looking for I break the silence between us.

"I didn't throw it out." I say around a lump in my

throat. "I just put it in a different pot. It was root bound."

Having a conversation with a man as hot as Alan while standing in my kitchen wearing a tank top and long basketball shorts was not part of my plan for today. I wanted to be comfortable while playing the new *Pirate's Lament* on my PlayStation last night and that meant a thin lightweight outfit that no one besides me would ever see. The top is stained with wine and paint from an abandoned project that I can't get out.

Not to mention that the guy who broke my heart and ruined my life is seeing me without a bra for the first time and my traitorous nipples are already hard.

"I didn't say anything. I wanted to but I didn't. I should have said something, anything. I just thought that if he were talking shit to me, he would leave you alone." Alan says, "It was stupid I know but I'm not ashamed of you, or of us. I've been in this one hundred percent from the beginning."

My silence only encourages him to continue.

"I'm all in, Jill. I told everyone at the office we were dating years ago. This has never been a joke to me. Not a prank. I want you to be my wife one day. I want us to date, to live together, and I want to love you." He looks down at the floor before he raises his eyes to meet mine, "I love you Jill and I have for years. I just never thought you could love me back. So, I teased you and I played office pranks on you. But always I loved you."

I can't say anything as he paces and rants across the linoleum flooring of my kitchen. The words can't scrape past my dry throat. Even if I could force them out Alan shows no intention of letting me get a word in edge wise.

"I reported Chad for sexual harassment and insubordination." Alan says with his hands on his hips as he reaches one end of the galley kitchen and spins to pace the other way. "What he said about you was completely inappropriate. He's already on his third strike and now they'll have to fire him. He should've been fired a long time ago if you ask me."

"Chad is being fired on Monday." I finally say. "It's the worst kept secret among the managers and human resources. Everyone knows."

Alan spins to face me, all the bluster he was building up gone in an instant.

"He sent a bunch of dick pics to the girls in payroll." I explain. "I think HR set a record with how fast they processed his final write up."

"Then," Alan says swallowing nervously, "I'll quit."

I start to interrupt but he waves me away, "You will never have to worry that I have an ulterior motive for having a relationship with you. You won't feel pressured to date me or worry what a breakup would do to our work."

The shine of hope is back in his eyes as he steps

towards me, taking my hands in his and rubbing the backs of my hands with his thumbs.

"Just give me a chance, Jill."

"Don't call me that!" I blurt and he reels back instinctively as I surge forward to grab the lapels of his suit jacket.

"Don't ever call me that." I say with an intensity that shocks even me.

"Okay, Sweetheart." Alan says in that deep rumble of his. The low timber sending butterflies into flight in my stomach.

"Don't quit." I say trying to keep my voice clear even as a sob threatens to bubble up, "I should've trusted you. Trusted in myself and my heart. I love you, Alan."

"You should always trust yourself." Alan says with a smirk and a sage nod, "We both know you're always right."

"Shut up and kiss me."

And he did.

Asking him to slip out of his suit jacket had him stripping in my kitchen in a mad rush. My giggle had him glaring at me as he whipped his belt off.

"Sweetheart." His warm amber eyes met mine in a heated blaze as he stopped removing his clothes and started working on mine.

"Kitchen table or bed." Alan said while leaning down

to nuzzle and nibble my neck. "You have ten seconds to decide where I'm going to fuck you, or I'll lay you down on the floor."

Brain blanking as Alan follows a trail down my chest until my tank top gets in the way. I don't manage to protest until after he rips it down the middle.

"Don't pretend like you care about it." Alan growls against my chest before he begins to tease my nipples.

"Table." I moan as he nips my pebbled flesh.

"Too late." Alan croons as sinks to his knees and yanks my shorts off. "You ran out of time."

"Oh no." I simper as I sit down on the floor and lay back to let Alan slide over my body. Pants and boxers gone his warm skin feels delicious against mine.

"Mock me and I'll punish you."

"Nothing you could do to me would be a punishment."

"Tomorrow you'll get no orgasms." He breathes as he settles his shoulders under my bent knees. "Not a single damn one."

"But it's a Monday." I protest even as his tongue flicks against my clit. "Mondays *suck* and orgasms will make it so much better."

"Too damn bad you just had to be a brat." He murmurs against my slick thigh where his lips press the lightest kisses. Alan's warm tongue lapping at my sensitive flesh is ticklish and I fight the urge to squirm away. "Would've loved to call into work sick and spend the day in bed with you."

His tongue returns to my dripping core, laving me with the broad side and taking his sweet time. The slow build of heat has me thrashing but my pleas and cries are ignored. Nothing I can do speeds up his movements, the infuriating pace is steady as I fall into madness.

And just when I'm on the edge and about to plunge into ecstasy, Alan pulls back and covers the length of my body with his own.

The sharpness of his smile has returned, and I know that I won't be making any demands in our bed for a long time to come.

"I promised myself that the next time we would come together." He says with a gleam in his eye.

Notching his head against my core he leans forward to kiss me as he slides the entire length of his cock deep into me. Alan groans against my lips as my heat grips him. With his cock fully seated I can't help but to grip his shoulders and wiggle my hips against his in a wordless plea to move.

"I never want to stop fucking you." He growls into my ear as he curls above me, his thrusts slow and steady in the same beat as his licks from before.

"I'll remember that tomorrow." I say arching my breasts into his mouth. His tongue flicks over my nipple as his mouth sucks the tip.

"Not even if you beg me." I barely hear him say as my body shudders as my climax sweeps over me like a warm wave of water. Pleasure seeps from every inch of skin but in the aftermath Alan's strokes have gained speed and I'm rapidly approaching the edge of ecstasy again as the hard length of his cock rubs against my inner walls. The aftershocks of my orgasm causing my muscles to clench him as his dark eyes catch mine. The molten amber pools pouring his soul into mine as every second slows down and I can soak in every ounce of love I see there. How I didn't see his own affection when it so closely mirrors mine, I'll never know.

Screaming his name and scratching my nails down his back as he seizes above me, I fill his warmth feel me as the last dregs of my orgasm milk him for every drop of his come.

We lay in a melted heap of body parts as we catch our breath and allow our bodies to cool.

"How are your knees?" I ask after a while, wincing at the thought of his knees and the damage my kitchen floor surely did to them.

"Keep being a brat and it'll be you on your knees." Alan retorts immediately with a playful pat to my hip. "On a serious note, next time the floor is off limits. Unless there is a very plush rug."

Alan spent the night and left early in the morning to get ready for work. But not before dragging me out of bed and pouring us both bowls of cereal. He told me over our breakfast that he thought about packing an overnight bag on Saturday night but didn't want to be presumptuous.

Sitting at my tiny kitchen table in nothing but his white undershirt as he spooned mouthfuls of cinnamon toast crunch into his mouth while wearing only a pair of boxers felt domestic. Like everything else didn't matter so long as we were together.

"Next time." I said.

"We talking airline carry on size or personal item?" He asked with a smirk knowing damn well he could carry a full set of luggage through my front door, and I would let him.

"Use your intuition." I said before tipping the bowl back and drinking the leftover milk.

The kiss that followed curled my toes and lit my soul on fire. I was three seconds away from crawling in his lap when he pulled back and tapped my nose.

"Remember our little talk last night?" He said with a crooked grin. "No orgasms for you."

Luckily, he had to leave right away to make it back to his apartment or else we both would have been late. Because if he hadn't left, I would have tied him to the bed until we were both boneless and satisfied.

Alan

I get to work early to make sure I could stop by human resources before Chad's termination. Miranda arrives, and I quickly wave her down to get the form I need. The email would get the ball rolling and an investigation started but I want to fill out an official report of sexual harassment. I make sure to include all the details as Miranda watches me with amusement in her eyes.

"He's already being fired." She says.

"I know, but I want it on record." I reply while checking my phone to get the exact date of the meeting.

"The king of harassment filling a harassment report?" Miranda asks.

"King of harassment?" I ask.

"Jill made you out to be a devil." Miranda croons.

"If Jill ever asked me to stop I would. Instead, she sinks to my level and gives as good as she gets."

And she holds me accountable. I'm not a good man, but I will be better. There are too many occurrences of Chad's behavior that I should've reported. Enough of the women have stepped forward to have him face disciplinary action but he should have been fired years ago.

That scarecrow comment didn't appear out of thin air.

I grab Michael and Henry on their way in to work, pulling them into an empty conference room. My friendship with both men has flourished through the years making our work relationship that much smoother. It's rare that I have to pull rank.

"Chad is being fired today." I immediately say.

"We know." Henry says after he and Michael share a look with each other.

"I am the only man who filed a report against him." I tell them.

The only response they give me is a pair of raised eyebrows from Henry and a puzzled frown from Michael.

"For those comments about Jill?" Henry finally asks.

"Yes." I reply. "But every man in this office has heard his comments about the women who work here. We've seen him harass them day in and day out."

Henry connects the dots before Michael. A sharp glint entering his brown eyes.

"You're holding us accountable." It's not a question.

"Going forward." I say nodding. "I'm going to help Miranda set up a presentation on workplace harassment next week. I'll also talk to Lucy and

Walter so that we show a united front in the meeting. From now on I want it to be clear that we are all accountable for making this a safe work environment."

"See something, hear something, say something." Michael mutters to himself raking his hand through his hair.

"Exactly." I agree.

Henry frowns crossing his arms in front of his chest.

"I encouraged Flora and Ashley to report him when I heard he sent them dick pictures. I shouldn't have left it at that. Should've reported him myself."

I clap him on the shoulder. He understands where we all went wrong. It clearly unsettles him as much as it does me.

"Going forward, we'll do better." I say before I leave them in the conference room.

I've worked in Jill's shadow for the last three years. She laid every piece of groundwork, finding the best way forward, and essentially handed me a road map. Now I finally feel like I'm bringing something new to the table. I can't change the past, but we can learn from it.

And I'm going to lead us into the future.

Jill

"I filled out the change of address form." I say as I walk into work.

Alan looks up from his computer. His eyes are tinted pink and there are visible bags underneath them. Despite our talk and the night we spent together, the strain of our fight still shows. But I expected this. Alan keeps his walls high but once they come down, he's immensely vulnerable.

Knowing that I hold the power to crush him, to break his heart leaves me breathless. But seeing his soft and squishy emotions reassures me that I can trust him with my own feelings. That I can trust him with every part of me. And he needs to know that I do trust him.

His deep amber eyes shine with love as he looks at me, and I begin to ramble. The words rushing out of my mouth like the faster I speak the quicker he will return to his confident and self-assured self. A grown man who can handle my demands and roll with my verbal punches.

"For you, obviously. I am not moving into an apartment when I have a perfectly good house with a ridiculously good interest rate on my mortgage."

He slowly pushes his chair back and stands as I continue my rant.

"Once we're married, I'll add you to the deed." I say as his large hands come up to cup my heated cheeks. My own hands smooth down his suit lapel, stroking the soft fabric right over his heart.

His eyes are dark with emotion as he finally breaks his silence.

"Oh? Now we're getting married?" His deep voice carries through the office, but I'm not worried about the whispers from our coworkers or the eyes I'm sure are watching everything unfold from every direction.

"By your logic we've been dating for three years already. I'm not waiting until year seven for a ring, Alan." A light smack to his chest accompanies my words. Like a stamp of approval on a work expense. My light tone belays the nervous twist in my stomach. That my proposal is too much too fast.

"Never thought I would get engaged on Valentine's Day. Look at you being romantic." Alan says teasingly.

The smile that stretches his lips is joyful and bright as he leans down to kiss me. My vision goes blurry as his lips meet mine. I hear clapping but it's muffled by Alan's hands that are woven into my hair. I don't care that we're in the office or that our coworkers are staring. They all thought we were together years ago.

"Understood." Alan says when we part to catch our breath. His voice is lighter than normal as he catches his breath. "Do you need me to submit that form to HR?"

"I've got it." I say with a smile. His own smile is back in full force, reaching his eyes and as always, he looks as neat as a hairpin. Except for his blue striped tie, which my wandering hands clearly found while we were kissing. Straightening his tie, I fiddle with it for a moment longer than necessary.

Another chaste kiss and I turn to go back to my own desk. "And Alan?" I call over my shoulder.

"Yes, Sweetheart?"

I take a moment to relish the nickname that I once found so demeaning. Now I know it was his way of claiming me all those years ago.

"Happy Valentine's Day." I say with a grin.

A week ago, I wouldn't have imagined myself engaged. And on the day of love itself no less. Already I can practically hear Miranda's squeals of joy. And Gabriella and Emma's gloating.

"Happy Valentine's Day, Sweetheart." He says before turning back to his desk, because we are at work after all and we're nothing if not professional. My proposal being an obvious exception.

I texted the group chat before I walked into work, and I can feel my phone vibrating in my purse. I'm sure that they are blowing my phone up with a million questions. Last they heard Alan was a rat bastard who was going to die in a trap befitting a rodent. I'm sure I gave them whiplash between Friday night and today, but I know in my heart that this is the right choice.

It took a long time to get here but now I know I'm right where I need to be.

My first task of the day is firing off an official email letting Miranda know that she can file that form. It's only after I click send that I realize I've fallen for one more of Alan's pranks.

He changed my email signature to read Jill Landrum instead of Jill Sweeny.

"Seriously?" I ask looking around my laptop to meet his amber eyes. He approaches my desk in a casual stroll with his hands tucked into the pockets of his slacks.

"You beat me to it." He says with a grin. "But I didn't want to ruin my surprise."

And then in front of everyone he pulls a black velvet box out of his pocket and sinks down to one knee beside me.

"I know you already made your demands, but will you, Jill Sweeny, do me the honor of marrying me?" He asks with a cheeky grin.

"Yes." I say with tears in my eyes. "But that is seriously the last time you're allowed to call me by my name."

"Deal, Sweetheart." He says before pressing a gentle kiss to my lips.

Epilogue

Jill

"They will love you. I swear." Alan whispers with his cheek pressed against my head and his arms wrapped around me from behind. "How could they not love the woman I love?"

He is so sure of his parents' approval. So confident and cocky and I'm a bundle of nerves.

"We got engaged before I met them." I mutter in protest.

"Worried my father won't give you my hand in marriage?" His attempt at a joke makes me laugh but the nervous energy doesn't abate even as I picture Alan in a Victorian era dress accepting suitors.

"We had a very tense work environment for many years. Are you sure you never spoke badly about anything I did to you?"

"Well," He begins with an audible sigh, "Yes I suppose I did."

"What did you tell them?" I turn on him in a flash, "I need to know so I can tell them my side."

"It's all water under the bridge." He tries to dismiss my worry, but I'm hooked like a fish on a line.

"Jello stapler?" I ask as he grabs our bags from the back of the rental car. "That time I convinced you we were wearing Halloween costumes to work? Or was it when I programmed your email to send all company emails into the spam folder?"

My anxiety builds as I consider every single prank I've ever pulled. Every clever move in our chess game comes back to haunt me as I view it from an outsider's perspective. They're going to see me as their treasured son's bully. Worse, they may view our relationship as a power imbalance.

"Jill." Alan says with a hint of exasperation coloring his tone, "I told them about you changing my email signature to read '*Adam Longhorn*' and how I didn't notice for an entire week. My dad still laughs whenever my mom brings it up. Which is every time I don't notice something new, she's done around the house."

"Oh, that's very mild for us."

"Exactly." He says grabbing my hand and leading me towards the front door of the cabin we're sharing with his parents for the week on the shore of Lake Allatoona "But please don't tell them how I retaliated."

"Alan Landrum, do you want me to lie to your mother?"

"No, just don't volunteer it."

"But she needs to know what a monster her son has become."

"No, she doesn't. I'm an angel and it's staying that way, Sweetheart."

"We'll see." Already the wheels are turning inside my head with ways to steer the conversation. I could comment on her curtains, letting her know that Alan told me she had just replaced the linens last month. Something his father made sure to tell him.

"Sweetheart." Alan's deep timber causes goosebumps to rise along my arms and neck. "Don't you dare."

I don't reply. I just give him a wide smile with the biggest and most innocent doe eyes I can manage. He doesn't buy into it for a second but that's the point. He knows I'm going to leverage this against him. I'll paint him the villain in front of his own family and watch as their idealized version of him burns to a crisp before their very eyes.

But even as we reach the porch and ring the doorbell, I know this is all going according to his plan. Distracting me with a good-natured sabotage plot is exactly what I needed to settle my nerves. Alan knows me better than anyone else.

"Alan and Jill are here, Roni!" A man with salt and pepper hair clipped close to his scalp hollers over his shoulder as he answers the door. He's like an older version of his son in a white button down and khaki slacks.

He's shorter than Alan with a slightly rounded belly but the same warm smile stretching into a grin as he pulls my fiancé in for a hug.

Before I can say hello, a tall woman darts around the pair and swoops down to latch her arms around me. I'm spun in three circles before she releases me.

"Finally, we get to meet you!" Alan's mother, Roni shouts with a wide smile. Her curly messy hair is at odds with her son's meticulously styled and groomed appearance. Dozens of bangles slide along her forearms and a large gemstone necklace hangs down the front of her bohemian dress.

"Hi, Roni. Can I call you Roni?" I ask as she peers down at me with the same warm amber eyes that I've grown used to loving. She's several inches taller than her son even in her flat tan sandals.

"For now, darling." She tugs me into the cabin as she leans down to whisper in my ear, "I hope in time you'll feel comfortable calling me Mom."

The lump in my throat swells unexpectedly as my vision blurs and I have to take a moment to push down the warm squishy feelings her words have brought to the surface.

"Maybe after we're married." I reply as we breeze through the cabin and Roni shows us to our bedroom, letting us settle in before we all regroup in the kitchen later.

"Of course, we've only just met." Roni says before she leaves us to get settled, "I just feel like I know you so well. Al has talked about you for *years*. Without fail he managed to bring you up at every holiday and family dinner. He had it *bad*."

"Years?" I ask as I watch Alan try to hide a wince. "Al?"

"Don't you dare." He growls pointing a finger at me sharply, "She's my mother and I have to tolerate her nicknames."

"Sounds familiar, *Sweetheart*." I say placing a light hand on his linen shirt sleeve.

"It's no secret that I take after my mother." He says with an eyeroll. "Don't even think of calling me-"

"Calling you what?" I interrupt him. "A mama's boy?"

He turns to me with a mocking expression. With a quick flick of his fingers his shirt collar is unbuttoned. Next go his cufflinks.

"You're such a fucking brat."

"No stop! It tickles." I cry as his hands go to my waist. He pins me down with his body weight as he drags the tips of his fingernails down my curves.

"Quiet now, Sweetheart." He breathes against the crook of my neck. The heat of his breath against my cool skin sends shivers down my spine raising goosebumps along my arms and neck. "Wouldn't want my parents to hear us. Would you?"

"Ugh." I complain pushing against his shoulders, "Moment ruined."

"Next time I'm not stopping because of your delicate sensibilities. So, you better behave."

"You better behave, or you'll be on your knees making me come twice before I let you even think about touching your cock."

"There is my bossy babe." He says before leaning in for a slow languid kiss. "I missed her."

"We need to join your parents."

"If you insist." He sighs before leaving me on the bed to change his clothing into something more causal for the lake. "Heads up but my parents are a bit more affectionate than most people would define as appropriate."

"I was kind of picking up a hippie vibe from your mom."

"Yes. Just don't call her a hippie to her face. She hates the term."

Alan grabs a pair of swimming trunks with a palm tree pattern while I consider which of the swimsuits I packed for the trip I want to wear. The black one piece does wonders for my curves but the bikini with the underwire support makes my breasts look fantastic. I almost decide to play it safe and go with the one piece but considering what I know about his parents I go with the bikini. It covers just as much of my bobbles and bits as the other, it just exposes my soft stomach.

"Are you sure you want to go swimming?" Alan asks me once I ask him to help me tie my top in place. "We could have so much more fun if we just stay in the room."

"This is a *family* vacation." I grumble. I wave the loose strings over my shoulder in a hurry up gesture and wait for him to begin tying the ends together before I add, "Save it for our honeymoon."

"We need to start planning the wedding."

"It sounds like so much work, honestly."

"I'll make lists and appointments. You just pick what you like, and I'll take care of scheduling."

"You'll do all that?"

"Well, yes. It's just a big party, right? We've thrown dozens of those. This will just be fancier and more expensive. I can offer design advice and mail invitations all day."

"I love you."

"Love you too, Sweetheart."

A moment later I feel a tugging at the strings holding my bottoms in place.

"Alan, are you undoing my swimsuit?"

"Sorry, not sorry." Alan says undoing the string holding my top in place. "I promise I tried to resist."

Soft lips caress my skin, trailing their way up my shoulder to my neck and up to my ear.

"I just started thinking of you in a white dress, putting on this act like you're a good girl and how much I'm going to enjoy taking it off you and making you beg for your husband's cock."

It was a long time before we went swimming.

Author's Note

Thank you so much for reading *Sweetheart*! If you enjoyed it, it would mean so much if you left a review!

Cinnamon Kissed is Gabriella's story and it's set two years before *Sweetheart* during Christmas. It's full of insta-love and has a memorable meet cute that is tooth achingly sweet.

Pumpkin Spiced Love is Emma's story and takes place in the fall. It's the spiciest one yet and my personal favorite.

Thanks again for reading and I hope to see you in the next one!

About The Author

Jacqueline Carmine

A southern transplant in Michigan, Jacqueline spends most of winter indoors writing about monsters, men, and the women who love them. She prefers insta-love over slow burn but loves a good groveling scene. She drinks energy drinks daily to keep up with her husband and three dogs and has never refused a good tiramisu. She adores all dogs, most cats, and plants that actually want to live.

Books In This Series

Holiday Sweet Treats

Cinnamon Kissed

Gabriella is thrilled to be celebrating her first Christmas in Atlanta after moving from the Midwest. She's been struggling to adapt to her new home, but Christmas has always been a bit magical for her and like always it brings her joy and peace. An embarrassing mix up lands her a date with the hottest CFO in the city and she's certain this Christmas will be the most magical yet.

Oliver doesn't care one way or another about the holiday or it's season of cheer slogan. He's been working in the family business for over a decade and isn't looking forward to another family dinner sitting across from his boss. But when he meets Gabriella, he finds himself warming to the holiday.

If you're looking for a holiday themed novella with insta-love and steam this is it. HEA guaranteed, No cheating or OWD.

Pumpkin Spiced Love

Emma wants kinky sex, but she hasn't been able to tell any of her ex-boyfriends about her secret desires. Enter the SoulConnect dating app. She finds the perfect man to indulge her mask kink just in time for Halloween. He's miles away in Crescent Ridge, Colorado while she lives in Atlanta, Georgia. She can visit him once, get it out of her system and go back home with none the wiser.

But what if she wants more than one night? Will she be able to convince Andrew to try long distance?

Andrew lives near Crescent Ridge, a small mountain town where the only way to meet a woman is online. Most of the men he knows have signed up for mail order brides, and while it seems to work out just fine for them, he's not going to marry a stranger. Then he matches with Emma on a dating app, a woman who shares his darkest fantasies but only wants a casual hookup.

He's hooked from the beginning, but she only wants casual, and he wants everything. Even if he can convince her to take a chance on a real relationship, she lives hundreds of miles away. Will he be able to let her go when it's time?

If you're looking for the perfect fall read look

no further. Fall festivals, pumpkin spice, and Halloween spookiness is here! It's a short novella with a touch of insta-love and a whole latte of steam!

Manufactured by Amazon.ca
Acheson, AB

16119035R00072